RAMONA
AND HER
FATHER

RAMONA
AND HER
FATHER

Beverly Cleary

illustrated by Alan Tiegreen

A YEARLING BOOK

A YEARLING BOOK
Published by
Dell Publishing Co., Inc.
1 Dag Hammarskjold Plaza
New York, New York 10017

Yearling ® TM 913705, Dell Publishing Co., Inc.

ISBN: 0-440-47241-5

Reprinted by arrangement with
William Morrow & Company, New York
Printed in the United States of America

May 1979

30 29 28

CW

Contents

RAMONA
AND HER
FATHER

1
Payday

"Ye-e-ep!" sang Ramona Quimby one warm September afternoon, as she knelt on a chair at the kitchen table to make out her Christmas list. She had enjoyed a good day in second grade, and she looked forward to working on her list. For Ramona a Christmas list was a list of presents she hoped to receive, not presents she planned to give. "Ye-e-ep!" she sang again.

"Thank goodness today is payday," remarked Mrs. Quimby, as she opened the refrigerator to see what she could find for supper.

"Ye-e-ep!" sang Ramona, as she printed *mice or ginny pig* on her list with purple crayon. Next to Christmas and her birthday, her father's payday was her favorite day. His payday meant treats. Her mother's payday from her part-time job in a doctor's office meant they could make payments on the bedroom the Quimbys had added to their house when Ramona was in first grade.

"What's all this yeeping about?" asked Mrs. Quimby.

"I'm making a joyful noise until the Lord like they say in Sunday school," Ramona ex-

plained. "Only they don't tell us what the joyful noise sounds like so I made up my own." *Hooray* and *wow*, joyful noises to Ramona, had not sounded right, so she had settled on *yeep* because it sounded happy but not rowdy. "Isn't that all right?" she asked, as she began to add *myna bird that talks* to her list.

"Yeep is fine if that's the way you feel about it," reassured Mrs. Quimby.

Ramona printed *coocoo clock* on her list while she wondered what the treat would be this payday. Maybe, since this was Friday, they could all go to a movie if her parents could find one suitable. Both Ramona and her big sister, Beezus, christened Beatrice, wondered what went on in all those other movies. They planned to find out the minute they were grown-up. That was one thing they agreed on. Or maybe their father would bring presents, a package of colored paper for Ramona, a paperback book for Beezus.

"I wish I could think of something interesting to do with leftover pot roast and creamed cauliflower," remarked Mrs. Quimby.

Leftovers—yuck!, thought Ramona. "Maybe Daddy will take us to the Whopperburger for supper for payday," she said. A soft, juicy hamburger spiced with relish, French fries crisp on the outside and mealy inside, a little paper cup of cole slaw at the Whopperburger Restaurant were Ramona's favorite payday treat. Eating close together in a booth made Ramona feel snug and cozy. She and Beezus never quarreled at the Whopperburger.

"Good idea." Mrs. Quimby closed the refrigerator door. "I'll see what I can do."

Then Beezus came into the kitchen through the back door, dropped her books on the table, and flopped down on a chair with a gusty sigh.

"What was that all about?" asked Mrs. Quimby, not at all worried.

"Nobody is any fun anymore," complained Beezus. "Henry spends all his time running around the track over at the high school getting ready for the Olympics in eight or twelve years, or he and Robert study a book of world records trying to find a record to break, and Mary Jane practices the piano all the time." Beezus sighed again. "And Mrs. Mester says we are going to do lots of creative writing, and I hate creative writing. I don't see why I had to get Mrs. Mester for seventh grade anyway."

"Creative writing can't be as bad as all that," said Mrs. Quimby.

"You just don't understand," complained

Beezus. "I can never think of stories, and my poems are stuff like, 'See the bird in the tree. He is singing to me.'"

"Tee-hee, tee-hee," added Ramona without thinking.

"Ramona," said Mrs. Quimby, "that was not necessary."

Because Beezus had been so grouchy lately, Ramona could manage to be only medium sorry.

"Pest!" said Beezus. Noticing Ramona's work, she added, "Making out a Christmas list in September is silly."

Ramona calmly selected an orange crayon. She was used to being called a pest. "If I am a pest, you are a rotten dinosaur egg," she informed her sister.

"Mother, make her stop," said Beezus.

When Beezus said this, Ramona knew she

had won. The time had come to change the subject. "Today's payday," she told her sister. "Maybe we'll get to go to the Whopperburger for supper."

"Oh, Mother, will we?" Beezus's unhappy mood disappeared as she swooped up Picky-picky, the Quimbys' shabby old cat, who had strolled into the kitchen. He purred a rusty purr as she rubbed her cheek against his yellow fur.

"I'll see what I can do," said Mrs. Quimby.

Smiling, Beezus dropped Picky-picky, gathered up her books, and went off to her room. Beezus was the kind of girl who did her homework on Friday instead of waiting until the last minute on Sunday.

Ramona asked in a quiet voice, "Mother, why is Beezus so cross lately?" Letting her sister overhear such a question would lead to real trouble.

"You mustn't mind her," whispered Mrs. Quimby. "She's reached a difficult age."

Ramona thought such an all-purpose excuse for bad behavior would be a handy thing to have. "So have I," she confided to her mother.

Mrs. Quimby dropped a kiss on the top of Ramona's head. "Silly girl," she said. "It's just a phase Beezus is going through. She'll outgrow it."

A contented silence fell over the house as three members of the family looked forward to supper at the Whopperburger, where they would eat, close and cozy in a booth, their food brought to them by a friendly waitress who always said, "There you go," as she set down their hamburgers and French fries.

Ramona had decided to order a cheeseburger when she heard the sound of her father's key in the front door. "Daddy, Daddy!"

she shrieked, scrambling down from the chair and running to meet her father as he opened the door. "Guess what?"

Beezus, who had come from her room, answered before her father had a chance to guess. "Mother said maybe we could go to the Whopperburger for dinner!"

Mr. Quimby smiled and kissed his daughters before he held out a small white paper bag. "Here, I brought you a little present." Somehow he did not look as happy as usual. Maybe he had had a hard day at the office of the van-and-storage company where he worked.

His daughters pounced and opened the bag together. "Gummybears!" was their joyful cry. The chewy little bears were the most popular sweet at Glenwood School this fall. Last spring powdered Jell-o eaten from the pack-

age had been the fad. Mr. Quimby always remembered these things.

"Run along and divide them between you,"
said Mr. Quimby. "I want to talk to your
mother."

"Don't spoil your dinner," said Mrs.
Quimby.

The girls bore the bag off to Beezus's room,
where they dumped the gummybears onto the
bedspread. First they divided the cinnamon-
flavored red bears, one for Beezus, one for
Ramona. Then they divided the orange bears
and the green, and as they were about to divide the yellow bears, both girls were suddenly aware that their mother and father were
no longer talking. Silence filled the house. The
sisters looked at one another. There was something unnatural about this silence. Uneasy,
they waited for some sound, and then their

parents began to speak in whispers. Beezus tiptoed to the door to listen.

Ramona bit the head off a red gummybear. She always ate toes last. "Maybe they're planning a big surprise," she suggested, refusing to worry.

"I don't think so," whispered Beezus, "but I can't hear what they are saying."

"Try listening through the furnace pipes," whispered Ramona.

"That won't work here. The living room is too far away." Beezus strained to catch her parents' words. "I think something's wrong."

Ramona divided her gummybears, one heap to eat at home, the other to take to school to share with friends if they were nice to her.

"Something is wrong. Something awful," whispered Beezus. "I can tell by the way they are talking."

Beezus looked so frightened that Ramona became frightened, too. What could be wrong? She tried to think what she might have done to make her parents whisper this way, but she had stayed out of trouble lately. She could not think of a single thing that could be wrong. This frightened her even more. She no longer felt like eating chewy little bears. She wanted to know why her mother and father were whispering in a way that alarmed Beezus.

Finally the girls heard their father say in a normal voice, "I think I'll take a shower before supper." This remark was reassuring to Ramona.

"What'll we do now?" whispered Beezus. "I'm scared to go out."

Worry and curiosity, however, urged Beezus and Ramona into the hall.

Trying to pretend they were not concerned about their family, the girls walked into the kitchen where Mrs. Quimby was removing leftovers from the refrigerator. "I think we'll eat at home after all," she said, looking sad and anxious.

Without being asked, Ramona began to deal four place mats around the dining-room table, laying them all right side up. When she was cross with Beezus, she laid her sister's place mat face down.

Mrs. Quimby looked at the cold creamed cauliflower with distaste, returned it to the refrigerator, and reached for a can of green beans before she noticed her silent and worried daughters watching her for clues as to what might be wrong.

Mrs. Quimby turned and faced Beezus and Ramona. "Girls, you might as well know. Your father has lost his job."

"But he liked his job," said Ramona, regretting the loss of that hamburger and those French fries eaten in the coziness of a booth. She had known her father to change jobs because he had not liked his work, but she had never heard of him losing a job.

26

"Was he fired?" asked Beezus, shocked at the news.

Mrs. Quimby opened the green beans and dumped them into a saucepan before she explained. "Losing his job was not your father's fault. He worked for a little company. A big company bought the little company and let out most of the people who worked for the little company."

"But we won't have enough money." Beezus understood these things better than Ramona.

"Mother works," Ramona reminded her sister.

"Only part time," said Mrs. Quimby. "And we have to make payments to the bank for the new room. That's why I went to work."

"What will we do?" asked Ramona, alarmed at last. Would they go hungry? Would the men from the bank come and tear down the new room if they couldn't pay for it? She had never thought what it might be like not to have enough money—not that the Quimbys ever had money to spare. Although Ramona had often heard her mother say that house payments, car payments, taxes, and groceries seemed to eat up money, Mrs. Quimby somehow managed to make their money pay for all they really needed with a little treat now and then besides.

"We will have to manage as best we can until your father finds work," said Mrs. Quimby. "It may not be easy."

"Maybe I could baby-sit," volunteered Beezus.

As she laid out knives and forks, Ramona wondered how she could earn money, too. She could have a lemonade stand in front of the house, except nobody ever bought lemonade but her father and her friend Howie. She thought about pounding rose petals and soaking them in water to make perfume to sell. Unfortunately, the perfume she tried to make always smelled like rotten rose petals, and anyway the roses were almost gone.

"And girls," said Mrs. Quimby, lowering her voice as if she was about to share a secret, "you mustn't do anything to annoy your father. He is worried enough right now."

But he remembered to bring gummybears, thought Ramona, who never wanted to annoy her father or her mother either, just Beezus, although sometimes, without even trying, she succeeded in annoying her whole family. Ramona felt sad and somehow lonely, as if she were left out of something important, because her family was in trouble and there was nothing she could do to help. When she had finished setting the table, she returned to the list she had begun, it now seemed, a long time ago. "But what about Christmas?" she asked her mother.

"Right now Christmas is the least of our worries." Mrs. Quimby looked sadder than Ramona had ever seen her look. "Taxes are due in November. And we have to buy groceries and make car payments and a lot of other things."

"Don't we have any money in the bank?" asked Beezus.

"Not much," admitted Mrs. Quimby, "but your father was given two weeks' pay."

Ramona looked at the list she had begun so happily and wondered how much the presents she had listed would cost. Too much, she knew. Mice were free if you knew the right person, the owner of a mother mouse, so she might get some mice.

Slowly Ramona crossed out *ginny pig* and

30

the other presents she had listed. As she made black lines through each item, she thought about her family. She did not want her father to be worried, her mother sad, or her sister cross. She wanted her whole family, including Picky-picky, to be happy.

Ramona studied her crayons, chose a pinky-red one because it seemed the happiest color, and printed one more item on her Christmas list to make up for all she had crossed out. *One happy family.* Beside the words she drew four smiling faces and beside them, the face of a yellow cat, also smiling.

2

Ramona and the Million Dollars

Ramona wished she had a million dollars so her father would be fun again. There had been many changes in the Quimby household since Mr. Quimby had lost his job, but the biggest change was in Mr. Quimby himself.

First of all, Mrs. Quimby found a full-time job working for another doctor, which was good news. However, even a second-grader could understand that one paycheck would not stretch as far as two paychecks, especially when there was so much talk of taxes, whatever they were. Mrs. Quimby's new job meant that Mr. Quimby had to be home when Ramona returned from school.

Ramona and her father saw a lot of one another. At first she thought having her father to herself for an hour or two every day would be fun, but when she came home, she found him running the vacuum cleaner, filling out job applications, or sitting on the couch, smoking and staring into space. He could not take her to the park because he had to stay near the telephone. Someone might call to offer him a job. Ramona grew uneasy. Maybe he was too worried to love her anymore.

One day Ramona came home to find her

father in the living room drinking warmed-over coffee, smoking, and staring at the television set. On the screen a boy a couple of years younger than Ramona was singing:

> Forget your pots, forget your pans.
> It's not too late to change your plans.
> Spend a little, eat a lot,
> Big fat burgers, nice and hot
> At your nearest Whopperburger!

Ramona watched him open his mouth wide to bite into a fat cheeseburger with lettuce and tomato spilling out of the bun and thought wistfully of the good old days when the family used to go to the restaurant on payday and when her mother used to bring home little treats—stuffed olives, cinnamon buns for Sunday breakfast, a bag of potato chips.

"That kid must be earning a million dol-

lars." Mr. Quimby snuffed out his cigarette in a loaded ashtray. "He's singing that commercial every time I turn on television."

A boy Ramona's age earning a million dollars? Ramona was all interest. "How's he earning a million dollars?" she asked. She had often thought of all the things they could do if they had a million dollars, beginning with turning up the thermostat so they wouldn't have to wear sweaters in the house to save fuel oil.

Mr. Quimby explained. "They make a movie of him singing the commercial, and every time the movie is shown on television he gets paid. It all adds up."

Well! This was a new idea to Ramona. She thought it over as she got out her crayons and paper and knelt on a chair at the kitchen table. Singing a song about hamburgers would not be hard to do. She could do it herself. Maybe she could earn a million dollars like that boy so her father would be fun again, and everyone at school would watch her on television and say, "There's Ramona Quimby. She goes to our school." A million dollars would buy a cuckoo clock for every room in the house, her father wouldn't need a job, the family could go to Disneyland. . . .

"Forget your pots, forget your pans," Ramona began to sing, as she drew a picture of a hamburger and stabbed yellow dots across the top of the bun for sesame seeds. With a million dollars the Quimbys could eat in a restaurant every day if they wanted to.

After that Ramona began to watch for children on television commercials. She saw a boy eating bread and margarine when a crown suddenly appeared on his head with a fanfare

—ta *da*!—of music. She saw a girl who asked, "Mommy, wouldn't it be nice if caramel apples grew on trees?" and another girl who took a bite of cereal said, "It's good, hm-um," and giggled. There was a boy who asked at the end of a weiner commercial, "Dad, how do you tell a boy hot dog from a girl hot dog?" and a girl who tipped her head to one side and said, "Pop-pop-pop," as she listened to her cereal. Children crunched potato chips, chomped on pickles, gnawed at fried chicken. Ramona grew particularly fond of the curly-haired little girl saying to her mother at the zoo, "Look, Mommy, the elephant's legs are wrinkled just like your pantyhose." Ramona could say all those things.

Ramona began to practice. Maybe someone would see her and offer her a million dollars to make a television commercial. On her way to school, if her friend Howie did not walk with her, she tipped her head to one side and said, "Pop-pop-pop." She said to herself, "M-m-m, it's good," and giggled. Giggling wasn't easy when she didn't have anything to giggle about, but she worked at it. Once she practiced on her mother by asking, "Mommy, wouldn't it be nice if caramel apples grew on trees?" She had taken to calling her mother Mommy lately, because children on commercials always called their mothers Mommy.

Mrs. Quimby's absentminded answer was, "Not really. Caramel is bad for your teeth." She was wearing slacks so Ramona could not say the line about pantyhose.

Since the Quimbys no longer bought potato chips or pickles, Ramona found other foods— toast and apples and carrot sticks—to practice good loud crunching on. When they had chicken for dinner, she smacked and licked her fingers.

"Ramona," said Mr. Quimby, "your table manners grow worse and worse. Don't eat so noisily. My grandmother used to say, 'A smack at the table is worth a smack on the bottom.' "

Ramona, who did not think she would have liked her father's grandmother, was embarrassed. She had been practicing to be on television, and she had forgotten her family could hear.

Ramona continued to practice until she began to feel as if a television camera was watching her wherever she went. She smiled a lot and skipped, feeling that she was cute and lovable. She felt as if she had fluffy blond curls, even though in real life her hair was brown and straight.

One morning, smiling prettily, she thought,

and swinging her lunch box, Ramona skipped to school. Today someone might notice her because she was wearing her red tights. She was happy because this was a special day, the day of Ramona's parent-teacher conference. Since Mrs. Quimby was at work, Mr. Quimby was going to meet with Mrs. Rogers, her second-grade teacher. Ramona was proud to have a father who would come to school.

Feeling dainty, curly-haired, and adorable, Ramona skipped into her classroom, and what did she see but Mrs. Rogers with wrinkles around her ankles. Ramona did not hesitate. She skipped right over to her teacher and, since there did not happen to be an elephant in Room 2, turned the words around and said, "Mrs. Rogers, your pantyhose are wrinkled like an elephant's legs."

Mrs. Rogers looked surprised, and the boys

and girls who had already taken their seats giggled. All the teacher said was, "Thank you, Ramona, for telling me. And remember, we do not skip inside the school building."

Ramona had an uneasy feeling she had displeased her teacher.

She was sure of it when Howie said, "Ramona, you sure weren't very polite to Mrs. Rogers." Howie, a serious thinker, was usually right.

Suddenly Ramona was no longer an adorable little fluffy-haired girl on television. She was plain old Ramona, a second-grader whose own red tights bagged at the knee and wrinkled at the ankle. This wasn't the way things turned out on television. On television grownups always smiled at everything children said.

During recess Ramona went to the girls' bathroom and rolled her tights up at the waist

43

to stretch them up at the knee and ankle. Mrs. Rogers must have done the same thing to her pantyhose, because after recess her ankles were smooth. Ramona felt better.

That afternoon, when the lower grades had been dismissed from their classrooms, Ramona found her father, along with Davy's mother, waiting outside the door of Room 2 for their conferences with Mrs. Rogers. Davy's mother's appointment was first, so Mr. Quimby sat down on a chair outside the door with a folder of Ramona's schoolwork to look over. Davy stood close to the door, hoping to hear what his teacher was saying about him. Everybody in Room 2 was anxious to learn what the teacher said.

Mr. Quimby opened Ramona's folder. "Run along and play on the playground until I'm through," he told his daughter.

"Promise you'll tell me what Mrs. Rogers says about me," said Ramona.

Mr. Quimby understood. He smiled and gave his promise.

Outside, the playground was chilly and damp. The only children who lingered were those whose parents had conferences, and they were more interested in what was going on inside the building than outside. Bored, Ramona looked around for something to do, and because she could find nothing better, she followed a traffic boy across the street. On the opposite side, near the market that had been built when she was in kindergarten, she decided she had time to explore. In a weedy space at the side of the market building, she discovered several burdock plants that bore a prickly crop of brown burs, each covered with sharp, little hooks.

Ramona saw at once that burs had all sorts of interesting possibilities. She picked two and stuck them together. She added another and another. They were better than Tinker-toys. She would have to tell Howie about them. When she had a string of burs, each clinging to the next, she bent it into a circle and stuck the ends together. A crown! She could make a crown. She picked more burs and built up the circle by making peaks all the way around like the crown the boy wore in the magarine commercial. There was only one thing to do with a crown like that. Ramona crowned her-self—ta-*da*!—like the boy on television.

Prickly though it was, Ramona enjoyed wearing the crown. She practiced looking surprised, like the boy who ate the margarine, and pretended she was rich and famous and about to meet her father, who would be driv-

ing a big shiny car bought with the million dollars she had earned.

The traffic boys had gone off duty. Ramona remembered to look both ways before she crossed the street, and as she crossed she pretended people were saying, "There goes that rich girl. She earned a million dollars eating margarine on TV."

Mr. Quimby was standing on the playground, looking for Ramona. Forgetting all she had been pretending, Ramona ran to him. "What did Mrs. Rogers say about me?" she demanded.

"That's some crown you've got there," Mr. Quimby remarked.

"Daddy, what did she *say?*" Ramona could not contain her impatience.

Mr. Quimby grinned. "She said you were impatient."

Oh, that. People were always telling Ramona not to be so impatient. "What else?" asked Ramona, as she and her father walked toward home.

"You are a good reader, but you are careless about spelling."

Ramona knew this. Unlike Beezus, who was an excellent speller, Ramona could not believe spelling was important as long as people could understand what she meant. "What else?"

"She said you draw unusually well for a second-grader and your printing is the best in the class."

"What else?"

Mr. Quimby raised one eyebrow as he looked down at Ramona. "She said you were inclined to show off and you sometimes forget your manners."

Ramona was indignant at this criticism. "I

49

do not! She's just making that up." Then she remembered what she had said about her teacher's pantyhose and felt subdued. She hoped her teacher had not repeated her remark to her father.

"I remember my manners most of the time," said Ramona, wondering what her teacher had meant by showing off. Being first to raise her hand when she knew the answer?

"Of course you do," agreed Mr. Quimby. "After all, you are my daughter. Now tell me, how are you going to get that crown off?"

Using both hands, Ramona tried to lift her crown but only succeeded in pulling her hair. The tiny hooks clung fast. Ramona tugged. Ow! That hurt. She looked helplessly up at her father.

Mr. Quimby appeared amused. "Who do you think you are? A Rose Festival Queen?"

Ramona pretended to ignore her father's question. How silly to act like someone on television when she was a plain old second-grader whose tights bagged at the knees again. She hoped her father would not guess. He might. He was good at guessing.

By then Ramona and her father were home. As Mr. Quimby unlocked the front door, he said, "We'll have to see what we can do about getting you uncrowned before your mother gets home. Any ideas?"

Ramona had no answer, although she was eager to part with the crown before her father guessed what she had been doing. In the kitchen, Mr. Quimby picked off the top of the crown, the part that did not touch Ramona's hair. That was easy. Now came the hard part.

"Yow!" said Ramona, when her father tried to lift the crown.

"That won't work," said her father. "Let's try one bur at a time." He went to work on one bur, carefully trying to untangle it from Ramona's hair, one strand at a time. To Ramona, who did not like to stand still, this process took forever. Each bur was snarled in a hundred hairs, and each hair had to be pulled before the bur was loosened. After a very long time, Mr. Quimby handed a hair-entangled bur to Ramona.

"Yow! Yipe! Leave me some hair," said Ramona, picturing a bald circle around her head.

"I'm trying," said Mr. Quimby and began on the next bur.

Ramona sighed. Standing still doing nothing was tiresome.

After what seemed like a long time, Beezus came home from school. She took one look at Ramona and began to laugh.

"I don't suppose you ever did anything dumb," said Ramona, short of patience and anxious lest her sister guess why she was wearing the remains of a crown. "What about the time you—"

"No arguments," said Mr. Quimby. "We have a problem to solve, and it might be a good idea if we solved it before your mother comes home from work."

Much to Ramona's annoyance, her sister sat down to watch. "How about soaking?" suggested Beezus. "It might soften all those millions of little hooks."

"Yow! Yipe!" said Ramona. "You're pulling too hard."

Mr. Quimby laid another hair-filled bur on the table. "Maybe we should try. This isn't working."

"It's about time she washed her hair anyway," said Beezus, a remark Ramona felt was entirely unnecessary. Nobody could shampoo hair full of burs.

Ramona knelt on a chair with her head in a sinkful of warm water for what seemed like hours until her knees ached and she had a crick in her neck. "Now, Daddy?" she asked at least once a minute.

"Not yet," Mr. Quimby answered, feeling a bur. "Nope," he said at last. "This isn't going to work."

Ramona lifted her dripping head from the sink. When her father tried to dry her hair, the bur hooks clung to the towel. He jerked the towel loose and draped it around Ramona's shoulders.

"Well, live and learn," said Mr. Quimby. "Beezus, scrub some potatoes and throw them in the oven. We can't have your mother come home and find we haven't started supper."

When Mrs. Quimby arrived, she took one

look at her husband trying to untangle Ramona's wet hair from the burs, groaned, sank limply onto a kitchen chair, and began to laugh.

By now Ramona was tired, cross, and hungry. "I don't see anything funny," she said sullenly.

Mrs. Quimby managed to stop laughing. "What on earth got into you?" she asked.

Ramona considered. Was this a question grown-ups asked just to be asking a question, or did her mother expect an answer? "Nothing," was a safe reply. She would never tell her family how she happened to be wearing a crown of burs. Never, not even if they threw her into a dungeon.

"Beezus, bring me the scissors," said Mrs. Quimby.

Ramona clapped her hands over the burs.

"No!" she shrieked and stamped her foot. "I won't let you cut off my hair! I won't! I won't! I won't!"

Beezus handed her mother the scissors and gave her sister some advice. "Stop yelling. If you go to bed with burs in your hair, you'll really get messed up."

Ramona had to face the wisdom of Beezus's words. She stopped yelling to consider the problem once more. "All right," she said, as if she were granting a favor, "but I want Daddy to do it." Her father would work with care while her mother, always in a hurry since she was working full time, would go *snip-snip-snip* and be done with it. Besides, supper would be prepared faster and would taste better if her mother did the cooking.

"I am honored," said Mr. Quimby. "Deeply honored."

Mrs. Quimby did not seem sorry to hand over the scissors. "Why don't you go someplace else to work while Beezus and I get supper on the table?"

Mr. Quimby led Ramona into the living room, where he turned on the television set. "This may take time," he explained, as he went to work. "We might as well watch the news."

Ramona was still anxious. "Don't cut any more than you have to, Daddy," she begged, praying the margarine boy would not appear on the screen. "I don't want everyone at school to make fun of me." The newscaster was talking about strikes and a lot of things Ramona did not understand.

"The merest smidgin," promised her father. *Snip. Snip. Snip.* He laid a hair-ensnarled bur in an ashtray. *Snip. Snip. Snip.* He laid another bur beside the first.

58

"Does it look awful?" asked Ramona.

"As my grandmother would say, 'It will never be noticed from a trotting horse.'"

Ramona let out a long, shuddery sigh, the closest thing to crying without really crying. *Snip. Snip. Snip.* Ramona touched the side of her head. She still had hair there. More hair than she expected. She felt a little better.

The newscaster disappeared from the television screen, and there was that boy again singing:

Forget your pots, forget your pans.
It's not too late to change your plans.

Ramona thought longingly of the days before her father lost his job, when they could forget their pots and pans and change their plans. She watched the boy open his mouth wide and sink his teeth into that fat hamburger with lettuce, tomato, and cheese hanging out of the bun. She swallowed and said, "I bet that boy has a lot of fun with his million dollars." She felt so sad. The Quimbys really needed a million dollars. Even one dollar would help.

Snip. Snip. Snip. "Oh, I don't know," said Mr. Quimby. "Money is handy, but it isn't everything."

"I wish I could earn a million dollars like that boy," said Ramona. This was the closest she would ever come to telling how she happened to set a crown of burs on her head.

"You know something?" said Mr. Quimby. "I don't care how much that kid or any other kid earns. I wouldn't trade you for a million dollars."

"Really, Daddy?" That remark about any other kid— Ramona wondered if her father had guessed her reason for the crown, but she would never ask. Never. "Really? Do you mean it?"

"Really." Mr. Quimby continued his careful snipping. "I'll bet that boy's father wishes he had a little girl who finger-painted and wiped her hands on the cat when she was little and who once cut her own hair so she would be bald like her uncle and who then grew up to be seven years old and crowned herself with burs. Not every father is lucky enough to have a daughter like that."

Ramona giggled. "Daddy, you're being silly!" She was happier than she had been in a long time.

3

The Night of the Jack-O'-Lantern

"Please pass the tommy-toes," said Ramona, hoping to make somone in the family smile. She felt good when her father smiled as he passed her the bowl of stewed tomatoes. He smiled less and less as the days went by and he had not found work. Too often he was just plain cross. Ramona had learned not to rush home from school and ask, "Did you find a job today, Daddy?" Mrs. Quimby always seemed to look anxious these days, either over the cost of groceries or money the family owed. Beezus had turned into a regular old grouch, because she dreaded Creative Writing and perhaps because she had reached that difficult age Mrs. Quimby was always talking about, although Ramona found this hard to believe.

Even Picky-picky was not himself. He lashed his tail and stalked angrily away from his dish when Beezus served him Puss-puddy, the cheapest brand of cat food Mrs. Quimby could find in the market.

All this worried Ramona. She wanted her father to smile and joke, her mother to look happy, her sister to be cheerful, and Picky-picky to eat his food, wash his whiskers, and purr the way he used to.

"And so," Mr. Quimby was saying, "at the

end of the interview for the job, the man said he would let me know if anything turned up."

Mrs. Quimby sighed. "Let's hope you hear from him. Oh, by the way, the car has been making a funny noise. A sort of *tappety-tappety* sound."

"It's Murphy's Law," said Mr. Quimby. "Anything that can go wrong will."

Ramona knew her father was not joking this time. Last week, when the washing machine refused to work, the Quimbys had been horrified by the size of the repair bill.

"I like tommy-toes," said Ramona, hoping her little joke would work a second time. This was not exactly true, but she was willing to sacrifice truth for a smile.

Since no one paid any attention, Ramona spoke louder as she lifted the bowl of stewed tomatoes. "Does anybody want any tommy-toes?" she asked. The bowl tipped. Mrs. Quimby silently reached over and wiped spilled juice from the table with her napkin. Crestfallen, Ramona set the bowl down. No one had smiled.

"Ramona," said Mr. Quimby, "my grandmother used to have a saying. 'First time is funny, second time is silly, third time is a spanking.'"

Ramona looked down at her place mat. Nothing seemed to go right lately. Picky-picky must have felt the same way. He sat down beside Beezus and meowed his crossest meow.

Mr. Quimby lit a cigarette and asked his older daughter, "Haven't you fed that cat yet?"

Beezus rose to clear the table. "It wouldn't do any good. He hasn't eaten his breakfast. He won't eat that cheap Puss-puddy."

"Too bad about him." Mr. Quimby blew a cloud of smoke toward the ceiling.

"He goes next door and mews as if we never give him anything to eat," said Beezus. "It's embarrassing."

"He'll just have to learn to eat what we can afford," said Mr. Quimby. "Or we will get rid of him."

This statement shocked Ramona. Picky-picky had been a member of the family since before she was born.

"Well, I don't blame him," said Beezus, picking up the cat and pressing her cheek against his fur. "Puss-puddy stinks."

Mr. Quimby ground out his cigarette.

"Guess what?" said Mrs. Quimby, as if to change the subject. "Howie's grandmother drove out to visit her sister, who lives on a farm, and her sister sent in a lot of pumpkins for jack-o'-lanterns for the neighborhood children. Mrs. Kemp gave us a big one, and it's down in the basement now, waiting to be carved.

"Me! Me!" cried Ramona. "Let me get it!"

"Let's give it a real scary face," said Beezus, no longer difficult.

"I'll have to sharpen my knife," said Mr. Quimby.

"Run along and bring it up, Ramona," said Mrs. Quimby with a real smile.

Relief flooded through Ramona. Her family had returned to normal. She snapped on the basement light, thumped down the stairs, and there in the shadow of the furnace pipes, which reached out like ghostly arms, was a big, round pumpkin. Ramona grasped its scratchy stem, found the pumpkin too big to lift that way, bent over, hugged it in both

67

arms, and raised it from the cement floor. The pumpkin was heavier than she had expected, and she must not let it drop and smash all over the concrete floor.

"Need some help, Ramona?" Mrs. Quimby called down the stairs.

"I can do it." Ramona felt for each step with her feet and emerged, victorious, into the kitchen.

"Wow! That *is* a big one." Mr. Quimby was sharpening his jackknife on a whetstone while Beezus and her mother hurried through the dishes.

"A pumpkin that size would cost a lot at the market," Mrs. Quimby remarked. "A couple of dollars, at least."

"Let's give it eyebrows like last year," said Ramona.

"And ears," said Beezus.

"And lots of teeth," added Ramona. There would be no jack-o'-lantern with one tooth and three triangles for eyes and nose in the Quimbys' front window on Halloween. Mr. Quimby was the best pumpkin carver on Klickitat Street. Everybody knew that.

"Hmm. Let's see now." Mr. Quimby studied the pumpkin, turning it to find the best side for the face. "I think the nose should go about here. With a pencil he sketched a nose-shaped nose, not a triangle, while his daughters leaned on their elbows to watch.

"Shall we have it smile or frown?" he asked.

"Smile!" said Ramona, who had had enough of frowning.

"Frown!" said Beezus.

The mouth turned up on one side and down on the other. Eyes were sketched and eyebrows. "Very expressive," said Mr. Quimby.

"Something between a leer and a sneer." He cut a circle around the top of the pumpkin and lifted it off for a lid.

Without being asked, Ramona found a big spoon for scooping out the seeds.

Picky-picky came into the kitchen to see if something beside Puss-puddy had been placed in his dish. When he found that it had not, he paused, sniffed the unfamiliar pumpkin smell, and with his tail twitching angrily stalked out of the kitchen. Ramona was glad Beezus did not notice.

"If we don't let the candle burn the jack-o'-lantern, we can have pumpkin pie," said Mrs. Quimby. "I can even freeze some of the pumpkin for Thanksgiving."

Mr. Quimby began to whistle as he carved with skill and care, first a mouthful of teeth, each one neat and square, then eyes and

71

jagged, ferocious eyebrows. He was working on two ears shaped like question marks, when Mrs. Quimby said, "Bedtime, Ramona."

"I am going to stay up until Daddy finishes," Ramona informed her family. "No ifs, ands, or buts."

"Run along and take your bath," said Mrs. Quimby, "and you can watch awhile longer."

Because her family was happy once more, Ramona did not protest. She returned quickly, however, still damp under her pajamas, to see what her father had thought of next. Hair, that's what he had thought of, something he could carve because the pumpkin was so big. He cut a few C-shaped curls around the hole in the top of the pumpkin before he reached inside and hollowed out a candle holder in the bottom.

"There," he said and rinsed his jackknife under the kitchen faucet. "A work of art."

Mrs. Quimby found a candle stub, inserted it in the pumpkin, lit it, and set the lid in place. Ramona switched off the light. The jack-o'-lantern leered and sneered with a flickering flame.

"Oh, Daddy!" Ramona threw her arms around her father. "It's the wickedest jack-o'-lantern in the whole world."

Mr. Quimby kissed the top of Ramona's head. "Thank you. I take that as a compliment. Now run along to bed."

Ramona could tell by the sound of her father's voice that he was smiling. She ran off to her room without thinking up excuses for staying up just five more minutes, added a postscript to her prayers thanking God for the big pumpkin, and another asking him to find her father a job, and fell asleep at once, not bothering to tuck her panda bear in beside her for comfort.

In the middle of the night Ramona found herself suddenly awake without knowing why she was awake. Had she heard a noise? Yes, she had. Tense, she listened hard. There it was again, a sort of thumping, scuffling noise, not very loud but there just the same. Silence. Then she heard it again. Inside the house. In the kitchen. Something was in the kitchen, and it was moving.

Ramona's mouth was so dry she could

barely whisper, "Daddy!" No answer. More thumping. Someone bumped against the wall. Someone, something was coming to get them. Ramona thought about the leering, sneering face on the kitchen table. All the ghost stories she had ever heard, all the ghostly pictures she had ever seen flew through her mind. Could the jack-o'-lantern have come to life? Of course not. It was only a pumpkin, but still— A bodyless, leering head was too horrifying to think about.

Ramona sat up in bed and shrieked, "Daddy!"

A light came on in her parents' room, feet thumped to the floor, Ramona's tousled father in rumpled pajamas was silhouetted in Ramona's doorway, followed by her mother tugging a robe on over her short nightgown.

"What is it, Baby?" asked Mr. Quimby. Both Ramona's parents called her Baby when they were worried about her, and tonight Ramona was so relieved to see them she did not mind.

"Was it a bad dream?" asked Mrs. Quimby.

"Th-there's something in the kitchen." Ramona's voice quavered.

Beezus, only half-awake, joined the family. "What's happening?" she asked. "What's going on?"

"There's something in the kitchen," said Ramona, feeling braver. "Something moving."

"Sh-h!" commanded Mr. Quimby.

Tense, the family listened to silence.

"You just had a bad dream." Mrs. Quimby came into the room, kissed Ramona, and started to tuck her in.

Ramona pushed the blanket away. "It was *not* a bad dream," she insisted. "I did too hear something. Something spooky."

"All we have to do is look," said Mr.

76

Quimby, reasonably—and bravely, Ramona thought. Nobody would get her into that kitchen.

Ramona waited, scarcely breathing, fearing for her father's safety as he walked down the hall and flipped on the kitchen light. No shout, no yell came from that part of the house. Instead her father laughed, and Ramona felt brave enough to follow the rest of the family to see what was funny.

There was a strong smell of cat food in the kitchen. What Ramona saw, and what Beezus saw, did not strike them as one bit funny. Their jack-o'-lantern, the jack-o'-lantern their father had worked so hard to carve, no longer had a whole face. Part of its forehead, one ferocious eyebrow, one eye, and part of its nose were gone, replaced by a jagged hole edged by little teeth marks. Picky-picky was crouched in guilt under the kitchen table.

The nerve of that cat. "Bad cat! Bad cat!" shrieked Ramona, stamping her bare foot on the cold linoleum. The old yellow cat fled to the dining room, where he crouched under the table, his eyes glittering out of the darkness.

Mrs. Quimby laughed a small rueful laugh. "I knew he liked canteloupe, but I had no idea he liked pumpkin, too." With a butcher's knife she began to cut up the remains of the jack-o'-lantern, carefully removing, Ramona noticed, the parts with teeth marks.

"I *told* you he wouldn't eat that awful Puss-puddy." Beezus was accusing her father of denying their cat. "Of course he had to eat our jack-o'-lantern. He's starving."

"Beezus, dear," said Mrs. Quimby. "We simply cannot afford the brand of food Picky-picky used to eat. Now be reasonable."

Beezus was in no mood to be reasonable. "Then how come Daddy can afford to smoke?" she demanded to know.

Ramona was astonished to hear her sister speak this way to her mother.

Mr. Quimby looked angry. "Young lady," he said, and when he called Beezus young lady, Ramona knew her sister had better watch out. "Young lady, I've heard enough about that old tom cat and his food. My cigarettes are none of your business."

Ramona expected Beezus to say she was sorry or maybe burst into tears and run to her room. Instead she pulled Picky-picky out from under the table and held him to her chest as if she were shielding him from danger. "They are too my business," she informed her father. "Cigarettes can kill you. Your lungs will turn black and you'll *die!* We made posters about it at school. And besides, cigarettes pollute the air!"

Ramona was horrified by her sister's daring, and at the same time she was a tiny bit pleased. Beezus was usually well-behaved while Ramona was the one who had tantrums. Then she was struck by the meaning of her sister's angry words and was frightened.

"That's enough out of you," Mr. Quimby told Beezus, "and let me remind you that if you had shut that cat in the basement as you were supposed to, this would never have happened."

Mrs. Quimby quietly stowed the remains of the jack-o'-lantern in a plastic bag in the refrigerator.

Beezus opened the basement door and gently set Picky-picky on the top step. "Nighty-night," she said tenderly.

"Young lady," began Mr. Quimby. Young lady again! Now Beezus was really going to catch it. "You are getting altogether too big for your britches lately. Just be careful how you talk around this house."

Still Beezus did not say she was sorry. She did not burst into tears. She simply stalked off to her room.

Ramona was the one who burst into tears. She didn't mind when she and Beezus quarreled. She even enjoyed a good fight now and then to clear the air, but she could not bear it when anyone else in the family quarreled, and those awful things Beezus said—were they true?

"Don't cry, Ramona." Mrs. Quimby put her arm around her younger daughter. "We'll get another pumpkin."

"B-but it won't be as big," sobbed Ramona,

who wasn't crying about the pumpkin at all. She was crying about important things like her father being cross so much now that he wasn't working and his lungs turning black and Beezus being so disagreeable when before she had always been so polite (to grown-ups) and anxious to do the right thing.

"Come on, let's all go to bed and things will look brighter in the morning," said Mrs. Quimby.

"In a few minutes." Mr. Quimby picked up a package of cigarettes he had left on the kitchen table, shook one out, lit it, and sat down, still looking angry.

Were his lungs turning black this very minute? Ramona wondered. How would anybody know, when his lungs were inside him? She let her mother guide her to her room and tuck her in bed.

83

"Now don't worry about your jack-o'-lantern. We'll get another pumpkin. It won't be as big, but you'll have your jack-o'-lantern." Mrs. Quimby kissed Ramona good-night.

"Nighty-night," said Ramona in a muffled voice. As soon as her mother left, she hopped out of bed and pulled her old panda bear out from under the bed and tucked it under the covers beside her for comfort. The bear must have been dusty because Ramona sneezed.

"*Gesundheit!*" said Mr. Quimby, passing by her door. "We'll carve another jack-o'-lantern tomorrow. Don't worry." He was not angry with Ramona.

Ramona snuggled down with her dusty bear. Didn't grown-ups think children worried about anything but jack-o'-lanterns? Didn't they know children worried about grown-ups?

4

Ramona to the Rescue

The Quimbys said very little at breakfast the next morning. Beezus was moody and silent. Mrs. Quimby, in her white uniform, was in a hurry to leave for work. Picky-picky resentfully ate a few bites of Puss-puddy. Mr. Quimby did not say, "I told you he would eat it when he was really hungry," but the whole family was thinking it. He might as well have said it.

Ramona wished her family would cheer up. When they had finished eating, she found herself alone with her father.

"Bring me an ashtray, please," said Mr. Quimby. "That's a good girl."

Reluctantly Ramona brought the ashtray and, with her face rigid with disapproval, watched her father light his after-breakfast cigarette.

"Why so solemn?" he asked as he shook out the flame of the match.

"Is it true what Beezus said?" Ramona demanded.

"About what?" asked Mr. Quimby.

Ramona had a feeling her father really knew what she meant. "About smoking will make your lungs turn black," she answered.

Mr. Quimby blew a puff of smoke toward the ceiling. "I expect to be one of those old men with a long gray beard who has his picture in the paper on his hundredth birthday and who tells reporters he owes his long life to cigarettes and whiskey."

Ramona was not amused. "Daddy"—her voice was stern—"you are just being silly again."

Her father took a deep breath and blew three smoke rings across the table, a most unsatisfactory answer to Ramona.

On the way to school Ramona cut across the lawn for the pleasure of leaving footprints in the dew and then did not bother to look back to see where she had walked. Instead of running or skipping, she trudged. Nothing was much fun anymore when her family quarreled and then was silent at breakfast and her father's lungs were turning black from smoke.

Even though Mrs. Rogers announced, "Today our second grade is going to have fun learning," as she wrote the date on the blackboard, school turned out to be dreary because the class was having Review again. Review meant boredom for some, like Ramona, because they had to repeat what they already knew, and worry for others, like Davy, because they had to try again what they could not do in the first place. Review was the worst part of school. Ramona passed the morning looking through her workbook for words with double *o*'s like *book* and *cook*. She carefully drew eyebrows over the *o*'s and dots within, making the *o*'s look like crossed eyes. Then she drew mouths with the ends turned down under the eyes. When she finished, she had a cross-looking workbook that matched her feelings.

She was in no hurry to leave the building at recess, but when she did, Davy yelled, "Look out! Here comes Ramona!" and began to run, so of course Ramona had to chase him around and around the playground until time to go inside again.

Running until she was hot and panting made Ramona feel so much better that she was filled with sudden determination. Her father's lungs were not going to turn black. She would not let them. Ramona made up her mind, right then and there in the middle of arithmetic, that she was going to save her father's life.

That afternoon after school Ramona gathered up her crayons and papers from the kitchen table, took them into her room, and shut the door. She got down on her hands and

knees and went to work on the bedroom floor, printing a sign in big letters. Unfortunately, she did not plan ahead and soon reached the edge of the paper. She could not find the Scotch tape to fasten two pieces of paper together, so she had to continue on another line. When she finished, her sign read:

NO SMO
KING

It would do. Ramona found a pin and fastened her sign to the living-room curtains, where her father could not miss it. Then she waited, frightened by her daring.

Mr. Quimby, although he must have seen the sign, said nothing until after dinner when he had finished his pumpkin pie. He asked for an ashtray and then inquired, "Say, who is this Mr. King?"

"What Mr. King?" asked Ramona, walking into his trap.

"Nosmo King," answered her father without cracking a smile.

Chagrined, Ramona tore down her sign, crumpled it, threw it into the fireplace, and stalked out of the room, resolving to do better the next time.

The next day after school Ramona found the Scotch tape and disappeared into her room to continue work on her plan to save her father's life. While she was working, she heard the phone ring and waited, tense, as the whole family now waited whenever the telephone rang. She heard her father clear his throat before he answered. "Hello?" After a pause he said, "Just a minute, Howie. I'll call her." There was disappointment in his voice. No one was calling to offer him a job after all.

"Ramona, can you come over and play?" Howie asked, when Ramona went to the telephone.

Ramona considered. Of course they would have to put up with Howie's messy little sister, Willa Jean, but she and Howie would have fun building things if they could think of something to build. Yes, she would like to play with Howie, but saving her father's life was more important. "No, thank you. Not today," she said. "I have important work to do."

Just before dinner she taped to the refrigerator door a picture of a cigarette so long she had to fasten three pieces of paper together to draw it. After drawing the cigarette, she had crossed it out with a big black X and under it she had printed in big letters the word *BAD*. Beezus giggled when she saw it, and Mrs. Quimby smiled as if she were trying not to smile. Ramona was filled with fresh courage. She had allies. Her father had better watch out.

When Mr. Quimby saw the picture, he stopped and looked while Ramona waited. "Hmm," he said, backing away for a better view. "An excellent likeness. The artist shows talent." And that was all he said.

Ramona felt let down, although she was not sure what she had expected. Anger, perhaps?

Punishment? A promise to give up smoking?

The next morning the sign was gone, and that afternoon Ramona had to wait until Beezus came home from school to ask, "How do you spell *pollution?*" When Beezus printed it out on a piece of paper, Ramona went to work making a sign that said, *Stop Air Pollution.*

"Let me help," said Beezus, and the two girls, kneeling on the floor, printed a dozen signs. *Smoking Stinks. Cigarettes Start Forest Fires. Smoking Is Hazardous to Your Health.* Ramona learned new words that afternoon.

Fortunately Mr. Quimby went out to examine the car, which was still making the *tappety-tappety* noise. This gave the girls a chance to tape the signs to the mantle, the refrigerator, the dining-room curtains, the door of the hall closet, and every other conspicuous place they could think of.

This time Mr. Quimby simply ignored the signs. Ramona and Beezus might as well have saved themselves a lot of work for all he seemed to notice. But how could he miss so many signs? He must be pretending. He had to be pretending. Obviously the girls would have to step up their campaign. By now they were running out of big pieces of paper, and they knew better than to ask their parents to buy more, not when the family was so short of money.

"We can make little signs on scraps of paper," said Ramona, and that was what they did. Together they made tiny signs that said, *No Smoking, Stop Air Pollution, Smoking Is Bad for Your Health,* and *Stamp Out Cigarettes.* On some Ramona drew stick figures of people stretched out flat and dead, and on one, a cat on his back with his feet in the air.

These they hid wherever their father was sure to find them—in his bathrobe pocket, fastened around the handle of his toothbrush with a rubber band, inside his shoes, under his electric razor.

Then they waited. And waited. Mr. Quimby said nothing while he continued to smoke. Ramona held her nose whenever she saw her father with a cigarette. He appeared not to notice. The girls felt discouraged and let down.

Once more Ramona and Beezus devised a plan, the most daring plan of all because they had to get hold of their father's cigarettes just before dinner. Fortunately he had tinkered with the car, still trying to find the reason for the *tappety-tappety-tap,* and had to take a shower before dinner, which gave the girls barely enough time to carry out their plan.

All through dinner the girls exchanged excited glances, and by the time her father asked her to fetch an ashtray, Ramona could hardly sit still she was so excited.

As usual her father pulled his cigarettes out of his shirt pocket. As usual he tapped the package against his hand, and as usual a cigarete, or what appeared to be a cigarette, slid out. Mr. Quimby must have sensed that what he thought was a cigarette was lighter than it should be, because he paused to look at it. While Ramona held her breath, he frowned, looked more closely, unrolled the paper, and discovered it was a tiny sign that said, *Smoking Is Bad!* Without a word, he crumpled it and pulled out another—he thought— cigarette, which turned out to be a sign saying, *Stamp Out Cigarettes!* Mr. Quimby crumpled it and tossed it onto the table along with the first sign.

"Ramona." Mr. Quimby's voice was stern. "My grandmother used to say, 'First time is funny, second time is silly—'" Mr. Quimby's grandmother's wisdom was interrupted by a fit of coughing.

Ramona was frightened. Maybe her father's lungs already had begun to turn black.

Beezus looked triumphant. See, we told you smoking was bad for you, she was clearly thinking.

Mrs. Quimby looked both amused and concerned.

Mr. Quimby looked embarrassed, pounded himself on the chest with his fist, took a sip of coffee, and said, "Something must have caught in my throat." When his family remained silent, he said, "All right, Ramona. As I was saying, enough is enough."

Ramona scowled and slid down in her chair.

Nothing was ever fair for second-graders. Beezus helped, but Ramona was getting all the blame. She also felt defeated. Nobody ever paid any attention to second-graders except to scold them. No matter how hard she tried to save her father's life, he was not going to let her save it.

Ramona gave up, and soon found she missed the excitement of planning the next step in her campaign against her father's smoking. Her afternoons after school seemed empty. Howie was home with tonsillitis, and she had no one to play with. She wished there were more children her age in her neighborhood. She was so lonely she picked up the telephone and dialed the Quimbys' telephone number to see if she could answer herself. All she got was a busy signal and a reprimand from her father for playing with the telephone

101

when someone might be trying to reach him about a job.

On top of all this, the family had pumpkin pie for dinner.

"Not *again!*" protested Beezus. The family had eaten pumpkin pie and pumpkin custard since the night the cat ate part of the jack-o'-lantern. Beezus had once told Ramona that she thought her mother had tried to hide pumpkin in the meat loaf, but she wasn't sure because everything was all ground up together.

"I'm sorry, but there aren't many pumpkin recipes. I can't bear to waste good food," said Mrs. Quimby. "But I do remember seeing a recipe for pumpkin soup someplace—"

"No!" Her family was unanimous.

Ramona was so disappointed because her father had ignored all her little signs that she did not feel much like eating, and especially not pumpkin pie for what seemed like the hundredth time. She eyed her triangle of pie and knew she could not make it go down. She was sick of pumpkin. "Are you sure you cut off all the parts with cat spit on them?" she asked her mother.

"Ramona!" Mr. Quimby, who had been stirring his coffee, dropped his spoon. "Please! We are eating."

They had been eating, but after Ramona's remark no one ate a bite of pie.

Mr. Quimby continued to smoke, and Ramona continued to worry. Then one afternoon, when Ramona came home from school, she found the back door locked. When she pounded on it with her fist, no one answered. She went to the front door, rang the doorbell, and waited. Silence. Lonely silence. She tried the door even though she knew it was locked. More silence. Nothing like this had ever happened to Ramona before. Someone was always waiting when she came home from school.

Ramona was frightened. Tears filled her eyes as she sat down on the cold concrete steps to think. Where could her father be? She thought of her friends at school, Davy and Sharon, who did not have fathers. Where had their fathers gone? Everybody had a father sometime. Where could they go?

Ramona's insides tightened with fear. Maybe her father was angry with her. Maybe he had gone away because she tried to make him stop smoking. She thought she was saving his life, but maybe she was being mean to him. Her mother said she must not annoy her

father, because he was worried about being out of work. Maybe she had made him so angry he did not love her anymore. Maybe he had gone away because he did not love her. She thought of all the scary things she had seen on television—houses that had fallen down in earthquakes, people shooting people, big hairy men on motorcycles—and knew she needed her father to keep her safe.

The cold from the concrete seeped through Ramona's clothes. She wrapped her arms around her knees to keep warm as she watched a dried leaf scratch along the driveway in the autumn wind. She listened to the honking of a flock of wild geese flying through the gray clouds on their way south for the winter. They came from Canada, her father had once told her, but that was before he had gone away. Raindrops began to dot the driveway, and tears dotted Ramona's skirt. She put her head down on her knees and cried. Why had she been so mean to her father? If he ever came back he could smoke all he wanted, fill the ashtrays and turn the air blue, and she wouldn't say a single word. She just wanted her father back, black lungs and all.

And suddenly there he was, scrunching through the leaves on the driveway with the collar of his windbreaker turned up against the wind and his old fishing hat pulled down over his eyes. "Sorry I'm late," he said, as he got out his key. "Is that what all this boohooing is about?"

Ramona wiped her sweater sleeve across her nose and stood up. She was so glad to see her father and so relieved that he had not gone away, that anger blazed up. Her tears became angry tears. Fathers were not supposed to worry their little girls. "Where have you been?" she demanded. "You're supposed to be here when I come home from school! I thought you had gone away and left me."

"Take it easy. I wouldn't go off and leave you. Why would I do a thing like that?" Mr. Quimby unlocked the door and, with a hand on Ramona's shoulder, guided her into the living room. "I'm sorry I had to worry you. I was collecting my unemployment insurance, and I had to wait in a long line."

Ramona's anger faded. She knew all about long lines and understood how difficult they were. She had waited in lines for her turn at the slides in the park, she had waited in lines in the school lunchroom back in the days when her family could spare lunch money once in a while, she had waited in lines with her mother at the check-out counter in the market, when she was little she had waited in long, long lines to see Santa Claus in the department store, and—these were the worst, most boring lines of all—she had waited in lines with her mother in the bank. She felt bad because her father had had to wait in line, and she also understood that collecting unemployment insurance did not make him happy.

"Did somebody try to push ahead of you?" Ramona was wise in the ways of lines.

"No. The line was unusually long today." Mr. Quimby went into the kitchen to make himself a cup of instant coffee. While he waited for the water to heat, he poured Ramona a glass of milk and gave her a graham cracker.

"Feeling better?" he asked.

Ramona looked at her father over the rim of her glass and nodded, spilling milk down her front. Silently he handed her a dish towel to wipe up while he poured hot water over the instant coffee in his mug. Then he reached into his shirt pocket, pulled out a package of cigarettes, looked at it a moment, and tossed it onto the counter. Ramona had never seen her father do this before. Could it be. . . .

Mr. Quimby leaned against the counter and took a sip of coffee. "What would you like to do?" he asked Ramona.

Ramona considered before she answered. "Something big and important." But what? she wondered. Break a record in that book of records Beezus talked about? Climb Mount Hood?

"Such as?" her father asked.

Ramona finished scrubbing the front of her sweater with the dish towel. "Well—" she said, thinking. "You know that big bridge across the Columbia River?"

"Yes. The Interstate Bridge. The one we cross when we drive to Vancouver."

"I've always wanted to stop on that bridge

and get out of the car and stand with one foot in Oregon and one foot in Washington."

"A good idea, but not practical," said Mr. Quimby. "Your mother has the car, and I doubt if cars are allowed to stop on the bridge. What else?"

"It's not exactly important, but I always like to crayon," said Ramona. How long would her father leave his cigarettes on the counter?

Mr. Quimby set his cup down. "I have a great idea! Let's draw the longest picture in the world." He opened a drawer and pulled out a roll of shelf paper. When he tried to unroll it on the kitchen floor, the paper rolled itself up again. Ramona quickly solved that problem by Scotch-taping the end of the roll to the floor. Together she and her father unrolled the paper across the kitchen and knelt with a box of crayons between them.

"What shall we draw?" she asked.

"How about the state of Oregon?" he suggested. "That's big enough."

Ramona's imagination was excited. "I'll begin with the Interstate Bridge," she said.

"And I'll tackle Mount Hood," said her father.

Together they went to work, Ramona on the end of the shelf paper and her father halfway across the kitchen. With crayons Ramona drew a long black bridge with a girl standing

112

astride a line in the center. She drew blue
water under the bridge, even though the Columbia River always looked gray. She added
gray clouds, gray dots for raindrops, and all
the while she was drawing she was trying to
find courage to tell her father something.

Ramona glanced at her father's picture, and
sure enough he had drawn Mount Hood
peaked with a hump on the south side exactly
the way it looked in real life on the days when
the clouds lifted.

"I think you draw better than anybody in the whole world," said Ramona.

Mr. Quimby smiled. "Not quite," he said.

"Daddy—" Ramona summoned courage. "I'm sorry I was mean to you."

"You weren't mean." Mr. Quimby was adding trees at the base of the mountain. "You're right, you know."

"Am I?" Ramona wanted to be sure.

"Yes."

This answer gave Ramona even more courage. "Is that why you didn't have a cigarette with your coffee? Are you going to stop smoking?"

"I'll try," answered Mr. Quimby, his eyes on his drawing. "I'll try."

Ramona was filled with joy, enthusiasm, and relief. "You can do it, Daddy! I know you can do it."

114

Her father seemed less positive. "I hope so," he answered, "but if I succeed, Picky-picky will still have to eat Puss-puddy."

"He can try, too," said Ramona and slashed dark V's across her gray sky to represent a flock of geese flying south for the winter.

5

Beezus's
Creative Writing

The Quimby women, as Mr. Quimby referred
to his wife and daughters, were enthusiastic
about Mr. Quimby's decision to give up smoking. He was less enthusiastic because, after
all, he was the one who had to break the habit.

Ramona took charge. She collected all her
father's cigarettes and threw them in the gar-

bage, slamming down the lid of the can with a satisfying crash, a crash much less satisfying to her father, who looked as if he wanted those cigarettes back.

"I was planning to cut down gradually," he said. "One less cigarette each day."

"That's not what you said," Ramona informed him. "You said you would try to give up smoking, not try to cut down gradually."

There followed an even more trying time in the Quimby household. Out of habit Mr. Quimby frequently reached for cigarettes that were no longer in his pocket. He made repeated trips to the refrigerator, looking for something to nibble on. He thought he was gaining weight. Worst of all, he was even crosser than when he first lost his job.

With a cross father, a tired mother, a sister who worried about creative writing, and a cat

117

who grudgingly ate his Puss-puddy, Ramona felt she was the only happy member of the family left. Even she had run out of ways to amuse herself. She continued to add to the longest picture in the world, but she really wanted to run and yell and make a lot of noise to show how relieved she was that her father was giving up smoking.

One afternoon Ramona was on her knees on the kitchen floor working on her picture when Beezus came home from school, dropped her books on the kitchen table, and said, "Well, it's come."

Ramona looked up from the picture of Glenwood School she was drawing on the roll of shelf paper taped to the floor. Mr. Quimby, who had a dish towel tucked into his belt for an apron, turned from the kitchen sink. "What's come?" he asked. Although it was

118

late in the afternoon, he was washing the breakfast dishes. He had been interviewed for two different jobs that morning.

"Creative writing." Beezus's voice was filled with gloom.

"You make it sound like a calamity," said her father.

Beezus sighed. "Well—maybe it won't be so bad this time. We aren't supposed to write stories or poems after all."

"Then what does Mrs. Mester mean by creative?"

"Oh, you know. . . ." Beezus twirled around on one toe to define creative.

"What are you supposed to write if you don't write a story or a poem?" asked Ramona. "Arithmetic problems?"

Beezus continued to twirl as if spinning might inspire her. "She said we should interview some old person and ask questions about something they did when they were our age. She said she would run off what we wrote on the ditto machine, and we could make a book." She stopped twirling to catch the dish towel her father tossed to her. "Do we know anyone who helped build a log cabin or something like that?"

"I'm afraid not," said Mr. Quimby. "We don't know anybody who skinned buffalo either. How old is old?"

"The older the better," said Beezus.

"Mrs. Swink is pretty old," volunteered Ramona. Mrs. Swink was a widow who lived in the house on the corner and drove an old sedan that Mr. Quimby admiringly called a real collector's item.

"Yes, but she wears polyester pant suits," said Beezus, who had grown critical of clothing lately. She did not approve of polyester pant suits, white shoes, or Ramona's T-shirt with Rockaway Beach printed on the front.

"Mrs. Swink is old inside the pant suits," Ramona pointed out.

Beezus made a face. "I can't go barging in on her all by myself and ask her a bunch of questions." Beezus was the kind of girl who never wanted to go next door to borrow an egg and who dreaded having to sell mints for the Campfire Girls.

"I'll come," said Ramona, who was always eager to go next door to borrow an egg and looked forward to being old enough to sell mints.

"You don't barge in," said Mr. Quimby, wringing out the dishcloth. "You phone and make an appointment. Go on. Phone her now and get it over."

Beezus put her hand on the telephone book. "But what'll I say?" she asked.

"Just explain what you want and see what she says," said Mr. Quimby. "She can't bite you over the telephone."

Beezus appeared to be thinking hard. "OK," she said with some reluctance, "but you don't have to listen."

Ramona and her father went into the living room and turned on the television so they couldn't overhear Beezus. When Ramona noticed her father reached for the cigarettes that were not there, she gave him a stern look.

In a moment Beezus appeared, looking flustered. "I meant sometime in a day or so, but she said to come right now because in a little while she has to take a molded salad to her lodge for a potluck supper. Dad, what'll I say? I haven't had time to think."

"Just play it by ear," he advised. "Something will come to you."

"I'm going too," Ramona said, and Beezus did not object.

Mrs. Swink saw the sisters coming and opened the door for them as they climbed the front steps. "Come on in, girls, and sit down," she said briskly. "Now what is it you want to interview me about?"

Beezus seemed unable to say anything, and Ramona could understand how it might be hard to ask someone wearing a polyester pant suit questions about building a log cabin. Someone had to say something so Ramona spoke up. "My sister wants to know what you used to do when you were a little girl."

Beezus found her tongue. "Like I said over the phone. It's for creative writing."

Mrs. Swink looked thoughtful. "Let's see.

123

Nothing very exciting, I'm afraid. I helped with the dishes and read a lot of books from the library. The *Red Fairy Book* and *Blue Fairy Book* and all the rest."

Beezus looked worried, and Ramona could see that she was trying to figure out what she could write about dishes and library books. Ramona ended another awkward silence by asking, "Didn't you make anything?" She had noticed that Mrs. Swink's living room was decorated with mosaics made of dried peas and beans and with owls made out of pine-cones. The dining-room table was strewn with old Christmas cards, scissors, and paste, a sure sign of a craft project.

"Let's see now. . . ." Mrs. Swink looked thoughtful. "We made fudge, and—oh, I know —tin-can stilts." She smiled to herself. "I had forgotten all about tin-can stilts until this very minute."

At last Beezus could ask a question. "How did you make tin-can stilts?"

Mrs. Swink laughed, remembering. "We took two tall cans. Two-pound coffee cans were best. We turned them upside down and punched two holes near what had once been the bottom of each. The holes had to be op-posite one another on each can. Then we poked about four feet of heavy twine through each pair of holes and knotted the ends to make a loop. We set one foot on each can, took hold of a loop of twine in each hand, and began to walk. We had to remember to lift each can by the loop of twine as we raised a foot or we fell off—my knees were always skinned. Little girls wore dresses instead of slacks in those days, and I always had dread-ful scabs on my knees."

Maybe this was why Mrs. Swink always

wore pant suits now, thought Ramona. She didn't want scabs on her knees in case she fell down.

"And the noise those hollow tin cans made on the sidewalk!" continued Mrs. Swink, enjoying the memory. "All the kids in the neighborhood went clanking up and down. Sometimes the cans would cut through the twine, and we would go sprawling on the sidewalk. I became expert at walking on tin-can stilts and used to go clanking around the block yelling, 'Pieface!' at all the younger children."

Ramona and Beezus both giggled. They were surprised that someone as old as Mrs. Swink had once called younger children by a name they sometimes called one another.

"There." Mrs. Swink ended the interview. "Does that help?"

"Yes, thank you." Beezus stood up, and so

did Ramona, although she wanted to ask Mrs. Swink about the craft project on the dining-room table.

"Good." Mrs. Swink opened the front door. "I hope you get an A on your composition."

"Tin-can stilts weren't exactly what I expected," said Beezus, as the girls started home. "But I guess I can make them do."

Do! Ramona couldn't wait to get to Howie's house to tell him about the tin-can stilts. And so, as Beezus went home to labor over her creative writing, Ramona ran over to the Kemps' house. Just as she thought, Howie listened to her excited description and said, "I could make some of those." Good old Howie. Ramona and Howie spent the rest of the afternoon finding four two-pound coffee cans. The search involved persuading Howie's mother to empty out her coffee into mayonnaise jars and calling on neighbors to see if they had any empty cans.

The next day after school Howie arrived on the Quimby doorstep with two sets of tin-can stilts. "I made them!" he announced, proud of his work. "And Willa Jean wanted some, so I made her a pair out of tuna cans so she wouldn't have far to fall."

"I knew you could do it!" Ramona, who had already changed to her playclothes, stepped onto two of the cans and pulled the twine loops up tight before she took a cautious step, lifting a can as she lifted her foot. First the left foot, then the right foot. *Clank, clank.* They worked! Howie clanked along beside her. They clanked carefully down the driveway to the sidewalk, where Ramona tried to pick up speed, forgot to lift a can at the same time she lifted her foot, and, as Mrs. Swink had recalled, fell off her stilts. She caught herself before she tumbled to the sidewalk and climbed back on.

Clank, clank. Clank, clank. Ramona found deep satisfaction in making so much noise, and so did Howie. Mrs. Swink, turning into her driveway in her dignified old sedan, smiled and waved. In a moment of daring, Ramona yelled, "Pieface!" at her.

"Pieface yourself!" Mrs. Swink called back, understanding Ramona's joke.

Howie did not approve. "You aren't supposed to call grown-ups pieface," he said. "Just kids."

"I can call Mrs. Swink pieface," boasted Ramona. "I can call her pieface any old time I want to." *Clank, clank. Clank, clank.* Ramona was having such a good time she began to sing at the top of her voice, "Ninety-nine bottles of beer on the wall, ninety-nine bottles of beer.

You take one down and pass it around. Ninety-eight bottles of beer on the wall. . . ."

Howie joined the singing. "Ninety-eight bottles of beer on the wall. You take one down and pass it around. Ninety-seven bottles of beer. . . ."

Clank, clank. Clank, clank. Ninety-six bottle of beer, ninety-five bottles of beer on the wall. Sometimes Ramona and Howie tripped, sometimes they stumbled, and once in a while they fell, muddying the knees of their corduroy pants on the wet sidewalk. Progress was slow, but what their stilts lost in speed they made up in noise.

Eighty-nine bottles of beer, eighty-six. . . . Ramona was happier than than she had been in a long time. She loved making noise, and she was proud of being able to count backwards. Neighbors looked out their windows to see what all the racket was about while Ramona and Howie clanked determinedly on. "Eighty-one bottles of beer on the wall. . . ." As Mrs. Swink had predicted, one of the twine loops broke, tumbling Ramona to the sidewalk. Howie knotted the ends together, and they clanked on until suppertime.

"That was some racket you two made," remarked Mr. Quimby.

Mrs. Quimby asked, "Where on earth did you two pick up that song about bottles of beer?"

"From Beezus," said Ramona virtuously. "Howie and I are going to count backwards all the way to one bottle of beer."

Beezus, doing homework in her room, had not missed out on the conversation. "We used to sing it at camp when the counselors weren't around," she called out.

"When I used to go to camp, we sang about the teeny-weeny 'pider who went up the water 'pout," said Mrs. Quimby.

The teeny-weeny 'pider song was a favorite of Ramona's too, but it was not so satisfying as "Ninety-nine Bottles of Beer," which was a much louder song.

"I wonder what the neighbors think," said Mrs. Quimby. "Wouldn't some other song do?"

"No," said Ramona. Only a noisy song would do.

"By the way, Ramona," said Mr. Quimby. "Did you straighten your room today?"

Ramona was not much interested in the question. "Sort of," she answered truthfully, because she had shoved a lot of old school artwork and several pairs of dirty socks under the bed.

❉   ❉   ❉

The next afternoon after school was even better, because Ramona and Howie had mastered walking on the tin-can stilts without falling off. "Sixty-one bottles of beer on the wall. Take one down and pass it around," they sang, as they clanked around the block. Ramona grew hot and sweaty, and when rain began to fall, she enjoyed the cold drops against her flushed face. On and on they clanked, singing at the top of their voices. Ramona's hair grew stringy, and Howie's blond curls tightened in the rain. "Forty-one bottles of beer on the wall. . . ." *Clank, crash, clank.* "Thirty-seven bottles of beer. . . ." *Clank, crash, clank.* Ramona forgot about her father being out of a job, she forgot about how cross he had been since he gave up smoking, she forgot about her mother coming home tired from work and about Beezus being grouchy lately. She was filled with joy.

The early winter darkness had fallen and the streetlights had come on by the time Ramona and Howie had clanked and crashed and sung their way down to that last bottle of beer. Filled with a proud feeling that they had accomplished something big, they jumped off their stilts and ran home with their coffee cans banging and clashing behind them.

Ramona burst in through the back door, dropped her wet stilts with a crash on the linoleum, and announced hoarsely, "We did it! We sang all the way down to one bottle of beer!" She waited for her family to share her triumph.

Instead her father said, "Ramona, you know you are supposed to be home before dark. It was a good thing I could hear where you were, or I would have had to go out after you."

Mrs. Quimby said, "Ramona, you're sop-

ping wet. Go change quickly before you catch cold."

Beezus, who was often embarrassed by her little sister, said, "The neighbors will think we're a bunch of beer guzzlers."

Well! thought Ramona. Some family! She stood dripping on the linoleum a moment, expecting hurt feelings to take over, perhaps even to make her cry a little so her family would be sorry they had been mean to her. To her wonder, no heavy feeling weighed her down, no sad expression came to her face, no tears. She simply stood there, cold, dripping, and feeling *good*. She felt good from making a lot of noise, she felt good from the hard work of walking so far on her tin-can stilts, she felt good from calling a grown-up pieface and from the triumph of singing backwards from ninety-nine to one. She felt good from being out after dark with rain on her face and the streetlights shining down on her. Her feelings were not hurt at all.

"Don't just stand there sogging," said Beezus. "You're supposed to set the table."

Bossy old Beezus, thought Ramona. She squelched off to her room in her wet sneakers, and as she left the kitchen she began to sing, "Ninety-nine bottles of beer on the wall. . . ."

"Oh, no!" groaned her father.

6

The Sheep Suit

Ramona did not expect trouble to start in Sunday school of all places, but that was where it was touched off one Sunday early in December. Sunday school began as usual. Ramona sat on a little chair between Davy and Howie with the rest of their class in the basement of the gray stone church. Mrs. Russo, the superintendent, clapped her hands for attention.

"Let's have quiet, boys and girls," she said. "It's time to make plans for our Christmas-carol program and Nativity scene."

Bored, Ramona hooked her heels on the rung of her little chair. She knew what her part would be—to put on a white choir robe and walk in singing carols with the rest of the second-grade class, which would follow the kindergarten and first grade. The congregation always murmured and smiled at the kindergarteners in their wobbly line, but nobody paid much attention to second-graders. Ramona knew she would have to wait years to be old enough for a chance at a part in the Nativity scene.

Ramona only half listened until Mrs. Russo asked Beezus's friend Henry Huggins if he would like to be Joseph. Ramona expected him to say no, because he was so busy training for the Olympics in about eight or twelve years. He surprised her by saying, "I guess so."

"And Beatrice Quimby," said Mrs. Russo, "would you like to be Mary?"

This question made Ramona unhook her heels and sit up. Her sister, grouchy old Beezus—Mary? Ramona searched out Beezus, who was looking pink, embarrassed, and pleased at the same time.

"Yes," answered Beezus.

Ramona couldn't get over it. Her sister playing the part of Mary, mother of the baby Jesus, and getting to sit up there on the chancel with that manger they got out every year.

Mrs. Russo had to call on a number of older boys before she found three who were willing to be wise men. Shepherds were easier. Three sixth-grade boys were willing to be shepherds.

While the planning was going on, a little voice inside Ramona was saying, "Me! Me!

What about me?" until it could be hushed no longer. Ramona spoke up. "Mrs. Russo, I could be a sheep. If you have shepherds, you need a sheep."

"Ramona, that's a splendid idea," said Mrs. Russo, getting Ramona's hopes up, "but I'm afraid the church does not have any sheep costumes."

Ramona was not a girl to abandon her hopes if she could help it. "My mother could make me a sheep costume," she said. "She's made me lots of costumes." Maybe "lots" was stretching the truth a bit. Mrs. Quimby had made Ramona a witch costume that had lasted three Halloweens, and when Ramona was in nursery school she had made her a little red devil suit.

Now Mrs. Russo was in a difficult position because she had told Ramona her idea was splendid.

"Well . . . yes, Ramona, you may be a sheep if your mother will make you a costume."

Howie had been thinking things over. "Mrs. Russo," he said in that serious way of his, "wouldn't it look silly for three shepherds to herd just one sheep? My grandmother could make me a sheep costume, too."

"And my mother could make me one," said Davy.

Sunday school was suddenly full of volunteer sheep, enough for a large flock. Mrs. Russo clapped her hands for silence. "Quiet, boys and girls! There isn't room on the chancel for so many sheep, but I think we can squeeze in one sheep per shepherd. Ramona, Howie, and Davy, since you asked first, you may be sheep if someone will make you costumes."

Ramona smiled across the room at Beezus.

They would be in the Nativity scene together.

When Sunday school was over, Beezus found Ramona and asked, "Where's Mother going to find time to make a sheep costume?"

"After work, I guess." This problem was something Ramona had not considered.

Beezus looked doubtful. "I'm glad the church already has my costume," she said. Ramona began to worry.

Mrs. Quimby always washed her hair after church on Sunday morning. Ramona waited until her mother had taken her head out from under the kitchen faucet and was rubbing her hair on a bath towel. "Guess what!" said Ramona. "I get to be a sheep in the Nativity scene this year."

"That's nice," said Mrs. Quimby. "I'm glad they are going to do something a little different this year."

145

"And I get to be Mary," said Beezus.

"Good!" said Mrs. Quimby, still rubbing.

"I'll need a sheep costume," said Ramona.

"The church has my costume," said Beezus.

Ramona gave her sister a you-shut-up look. Beezus smiled serenely. Ramona hoped she wasn't going to start acting like Mary already.

Mrs. Quimby stopped rubbing to look at Ramona. "And where are you going to get this sheep costume?" she asked.

Ramona felt very small. "I—I thought you could make me a sheep suit."

"When?"

Ramona felt even smaller. "After work?"

Mrs. Quimby sighed. "Ramona, I don't like to disappoint you, but I'm tired when I come home from work. I don't have time to do a lot of sewing. A sheep suit would be a lot of work and mean a lot of little pieces to put together,

146

and I don't even know if I could find a sheep pattern."

Mr. Quimby joined in the conversation. That was the trouble with a father with time on his hands. He always had time for other people's arguments. "Ramona," he said, "you know better than to involve other people in work without asking first."

Ramona wished her father could sew. He had plenty of time. "Maybe Howie's grandmother could make me a costume, too," she suggested.

"We can't ask favors like that," said Mrs. Quimby, "and besides material costs money, and with Christmas coming and all we don't have a nickel to spare."

Ramona knew all this. She simply hadn't thought; she had wanted to be a sheep so much. She gulped and sniffed and tried to

147

wiggle her toes inside her shoes. Her feet were growing and her shoes felt tight. She was glad she had not mentioned this to her mother. She would never get a costume if they had to buy shoes.

Mrs. Quimby draped the towel around her shoulders and reached for her comb.

"I can't be a sheep without a costume." Ramona sniffed again. She would gladly suffer tight shoes if she could have a costume instead.

"It's your own fault," said Mr. Quimby. "You should have thought."

Ramona now wished she had waited until after Christmas to persuade her father to give up smoking. Then maybe he would be nice to his little girl when she needed a sheep costume.

Mrs. Quimby pulled the comb through her

tangled hair. "I'll see what I can do," she said. "We have that old white terry-cloth bathrobe with the sleeve seams that pulled out. It's pretty shabby, but if I bleached it, I might be able to do something with it."

Ramona stopped sniffing. Her mother would try to make everything all right, but Ramona was not going to risk telling about her tight shoes in case she couldn't make a costume out of the bathrobe and needed to buy material.

That evening, after Ramona had gone to bed, she heard her mother and father in their bedroom talking in those low, serious voices that so often meant that they were talking about her. She slipped out of bed and knelt on the floor with her ear against the furnace outlet to see if she could catch their words.

Her father's voice, coming through the furnace pipes, sounded hollow and far away.

"Why did you give in to her?" he was asking. "She had no business saying you would make her a sheep costume without asking first. She has to learn sometime."

I have learned, thought Ramona indignantly. Her father did not have to talk this way about her behind her back.

"I know," answered Ramona's mother in a voice also sounding hollow and far away. "But she's little, and these things are so important to her. I'll manage somehow."

"We don't want a spoiled brat on our hands," said Ramona's father.

"But it's Christmas," said Mrs. Quimby, "and Christmas is going to be slim enough this year."

Comforted by her mother but angry at her father, Ramona climbed back into bed. Spoiled brat! So that was what her father thought of her.

The days that followed were difficult for Ramona, who was now cross with her cross father. He was *mean,* talking about her behind her back that way.

"Well, what's eating you?" he finally asked Ramona.

"Nothing." Ramona scowled. She could not tell him why she was angry without admitting she had eavesdropped.

And then there was Beezus, who went

151

around smiling and looking serene, perhaps because Mrs. Mester had given her an A on her creative-writing composition and read it aloud to the class, but more likely because she was practicing for her part as Mary. Having a sister who tried to act like the Virgin Mary was not easy for a girl who felt as Ramona did.

And the costume. Mrs. Quimby found time to bleach the old bathrobe in the washing machine, but after that nothing happened. The doctor she worked for was so busy because of all the earaches, sore throats, and flu that came with winter weather that she was late coming home every evening.

On top of that, Ramona had to spend two afternoons watching Howie's grandmother sew on his sheep suit, because arrangements had now been made for Ramona to go to Howie's house if Mr. Quimby could not be

152

home after school. This week he had to collect unemployment insurance and take a civil-service examination for a job in the post office.

Ramona studied Howie's sheep suit, which was made out of fluffy white acrylic. The ears were lined with pink, and Mrs. Kemp was going to put a zipper down the front. The costume was beautiful, soft and furry. Ramona longed to rub her cheek against it, hug it, take it to bed with her.

"And when I finish Howie's costume, I am going to make another for Willa Jean," said Mrs. Kemp. "Willa Jean wants one, too."

This was almost too much for Ramona to bear. Besides, her shoes felt tighter than ever. She looked at Willa Jean, who was clomping around the house on her little tuna-can stilts. Messy little Willa Jean in a beautiful sheep suit she didn't even need. She would only spoil the furry cloth by dribbling apple juice down the front and spilling graham-cracker crumbs all over it. People said Willa Jean behaved just the way Ramona used to, but Ramona could not believe them.

A week before the Christmas program Mrs. Quimby managed to find time to buy a pattern during her lunch hour, but she did not find time to sew for Ramona.

Mr. Quimby, on the other hand, had plenty of time for Ramona. Too much, she was begining to think. He nagged. Ramona should sit up closer to the table so she wouldn't spill so much. She should stop making rivers in her mashed potatoes. She should wring out her washcloth instead of leaving it sopping in the tub. Look at the circle of rust her tin-can stilts had left on the kitchen floor. Couldn't she be more careful? She should fold her bath towel in half and hang it up straight. How did she expect it to dry when it was all wadded up, for Pete's sake? She found a sign in her room that said, *A Messy Room Is Hazardous to Your Health.* That was too much.

Ramona marched out to the garage where her father was oiling the lawnmower so it would be ready when spring came and said, "A messy room is not hazardous to my health. It's not the same as smoking."

"You could trip and break your arm," her father pointed out.

Ramona had an answer. "I always turn on the light or sort of feel along the floor with my feet."

"You could smother in old school papers, stuffed animals, and hula hoops if the mess gets deep enough," said her father and added, "Miss Radar Feet."

155

Ramona smiled. "Daddy, you're just being silly again. Nobody ever smothered in a hula hoop."

"You never can tell," said her father. "There is always a first time."

Ramona and her father got along better for a while after that, and then came the terrible afternoon when Ramona came home from school to find her father closing the living-room windows, which had been wide open even though the day was raw and windy. There was a faint smell of cigarette smoke in the room.

"Why there's Henry running down the street," said Mr. Quimby, his back to Ramona. "He may make it to the Olympics, but that old dog of his won't."

"Daddy," said Ramona. Her father turned. Ramona looked him in the eye. "You *cheated!*"

156

Mr. Quimby closed the last window. "What are you talking about?"

"You smoked and you *promised* you wouldn't!" Ramona felt as if she were the grown-up and he were the child.

Mr. Quimby sat down on the couch and leaned back as if he were very, very tired, which made some of the anger drain out of Ramona. "Ramona," he said, "it isn't easy to break a bad habit. I ran across one cigarette, an old stale cigarette, in my raincoat pocket and thought it might help if I smoked just one. I'm trying. I'm really trying."

Hearing her father speak this way, as if she really was a grown-up, melted the last of Ramona's anger. She turned into a seven-year-old again and climbed on the couch to lean against her father. After a few moments of silence, she whispered, "I love you, Daddy."

He tousled her hair affectionately and said, "I know you do. That's why you want me to stop smoking, and I love you, too."

"Even if I'm a brat sometimes?"

"Even if you're a brat sometimes."

Ramona thought awhile before she sat up and said, "Then why can't we be a happy family?"

For some reason Mr. Quimby smiled. "I have news for you, Ramona," he said. "We *are* a happy family."

"We are?" Ramona was skeptical.

"Yes, we are." Mr. Quimby was positive. "No family is perfect. Get that idea out of your head. And nobody is perfect either. All we can do is work at it. And we do."

Ramona tried to wiggle her toes inside her shoes and considered what her father had said. Lots of fathers wouldn't draw pictures

with their little girls. Her father bought her paper and crayons when he could afford them. Lots of mothers wouldn't step over a picture that spread across the kitchen floor while cooking supper. Ramona knew mothers who would scold and say, "Pick that up. Can't you see I'm trying to get supper?" Lots of big sisters wouldn't let their little sister go along when they interviewed someone for creative writing. They would take more than their fair share of gummybears because they were bigger and . . . .

Ramona decided her father was probably right, but she couldn't help feeling they would be a happier family if her mother could find time to sew that sheep costume. There wasn't much time left.

7

Ramona and the
Three Wise Persons

Suddenly, a few days before Christmas when the Quimby family least expected it, the telephone rang for Ramona's father. He had a job! The morning after New Year's Day he was to report for training as a checker in a chain of supermarkets. The pay was good, he would have to work some evenings, and maybe someday he would get to manage a market!

After that telephone call Mr. Quimby stopped reaching for cigarettes that were not there and began to whistle as he ran the vacuum cleaner and folded the clothes from the dryer. The worried frown disappeared from Mrs. Quimby's forehead. Beezus looked even more calm and serene. Ramona, however, made a mistake. She told her mother about her tight shoes. Mrs. Quimby then wasted a Saturday afternoon shopping for shoes when she could have been sewing on Ramona's costume. As a result, when they drove to church the night of the Christmas-carol program, Ramona was the only unhappy member of the family.

Mr. Quimby sang as he drove:

"There's a little wheel a-turning in my heart.
There's a little wheel a-turning in my heart."

Ramona loved that song because it made

her think of Howie, who liked machines. Tonight, however, she was determined not to
enjoy her father's singing.

Rain blew against the car, headlights shone
on the pavement, the windshield wipers *splip-*

splopped. Mrs. Quimby leaned back, tired but relaxed. Beezus smiled her gentle Virgin Mary smile that Ramona had found so annoying for the past three weeks.

Ramona sulked. Someplace above those cold, wet clouds the very same star was shining that had guided the Three Wise Men to Bethlehem. On a night like this they never would have made it.

Mr. Quimby sang on, "Oh, I feel like shouting in my heart. . . ."

Ramona interrupted her father's song. "I don't care what anybody says," she burst out. "If I can't be a good sheep, I am not going to be a sheep at all." She yanked off the white terry-cloth headdress with pink-lined ears that she was wearing and stuffed it into the pocket of her car coat. She started to pull her father's rolled-down socks from her hands because they didn't really look like hooves, but then she decided they kept her hands warm. She squirmed on the lumpy terry-cloth tail sewn to the seat of her pajamas. Ramona could not pretend that faded pajamas printed with an army of pink rabbits, half of them upside down, made her look like a sheep, and Ramona was usually good at pretending.

Mrs. Quimby's voice was tired. "Ramona, your tail and headdress were all I could manage, and I had to stay up late last night to finish those. I simply don't have time for complicated sewing."

Ramona knew that. Her family had been telling her so for the past three weeks.

"A sheep should be wooly," said Ramona. "A sheep should not be printed with pink bunnies."

"You can be a sheep that has been shorn,"

165

said Mr. Quimby, who was full of jokes now that he was going to work again. "Or how about a wolf in sheep's clothing?"

"You just want me to be miserable," said Ramona, not appreciating her father's humor and feeling that everyone in her family should be miserable because she was.

"She's worn out," said Mrs. Quimby, as if Ramona could not hear. "It's so hard to wait for Christmas at her age."

Ramona raised her voice. "I am *not* worn out! You know sheep don't wear pajamas."

"That's show biz," said Mr. Quimby.

"Daddy!" Beezus-Mary was shocked. "It's church!"

"And don't forget, Ramona," said Mr. Quimby, "as my grandmother would have said, 'Those pink bunnies will never be noticed from a trotting horse.'"

166

Ramona disliked her father's grandmother even more. Besides, nobody rode trotting horses in church.

The sight of light shining through the stained-glass window of the big stone church diverted Ramona for a moment. The window looked beautiful, as if it were made of jewels.

Mr. Quimby backed the car into a parking space. "Ho-ho-ho!" he said, as he turned off the ignition. " 'Tis the season to be jolly."

Jolly was the last thing Ramona was going to be. Leaving the car, she stooped down inside her car coat to hide as many rabbits as possible. Black branches clawed at the sky, and the wind was raw.

"Stand up straight," said Ramona's heartless father.

"I'll get wet," said Ramona. "I might catch cold, and then you'd be sorry."

"Run between the drops," said Mr. Quimby.

"They're too close together," answered Ramona.

"Oh, you two," said Mrs. Quimby with a tired little laugh, as she backed out of the car and tried to open her umbrella at the same time.

"I will not be in it," Ramona defied her family once and for all. "They can give the program without me."

Her father's answer was a surprise. "Suit yourself," he said. "You're not going to spoil our evening."

Mrs. Quimby gave the seat of Ramona's pajamas an affectionate pat. "Run along, little lamb, wagging your tail behind you."

Ramona walked stiff-legged so that her tail would not wag.

At the church door the family parted, the

girls going downstairs to the Sunday-school room, which was a confusion of chattering children piling coats and raincoats on chairs. Ramona found a corner behind the Christmas tree, where Santa would pass out candy canes after the program. She sat down on the floor with her car coat pulled over her bent knees.

Through the branches Ramona watched carolers putting on their white robes. Girls were tying tinsel around one another's heads while Mrs. Russo searched out boys and tied tinsel around their heads, too. "It's all right for boys to wear tinsel," Mrs. Russo assured them. Some looked as if they were not certain they believed her.

One boy climbed on a chair. "I'm an angel. Watch me fly," he announced and jumped off, flapping the wide sleeves of his choir robe. All the carolers turned into flapping angels.

Nobody noticed Ramona. Everyone was having too much fun. Shepherds found their cloaks, which were made from old cotton bedspreads. Beezus's friend, Henry Huggins, arrived and put on the dark robe he was to wear in the part of Joseph.

The other two sheep appeared. Howie's acrylic sheep suit, with the zipper on the front, was as thick and as fluffy as Ramona knew it would be. Ramona longed to pet Howie; he looked so soft. Davy's flannel suit was fastened with safety pins, and there was something wrong about the ears. If his tail had been longer, he could have passed for a kitten, but he did not seem to mind. Both boys wore brown mittens. Davy, who was a thin little sheep, jumped up and down to make his tail wag, which surprised Ramona. At school he was always so shy. Maybe he felt brave inside his sheep suit. Howie, a chunky sheep, made his tail wag, too. My ears are as good as theirs, Ramona told herself. The floor felt cold through the seat of her thin pajamas.

"Look at the little lambs!" cried an angel. "Aren't they darling?"

"Ba-a, ba-a!" bleated Davy and Howie.

Ramona longed to be there with them, jumping and ba-a-ing and wagging her tail, too. Maybe the faded rabbits didn't show as much as she had thought. She sat hunched and miserable. She had told her father she would *not* be a sheep, and she couldn't back down now. She hoped God was too busy to notice her, and then she changed her mind. Please, God, prayed Ramona, in case He wasn't too busy to listen to a miserable little sheep, I don't really mean to be horrid. It just works out that way. She was frightened, she discovered, for when the program began, she would be left alone in the church basement. The lights might even be turned out, a scary thought, for the big stone church filled Ramona with awe, and she did not want to be left alone in the dark with her awe. Please, God, prayed Ramona, get me out of this mess.

Beezus, in a long blue robe with a white scarf over her head and carrying a baby's blanket and a big flashlight, found her little sister. "Come out, Ramona," she coaxed. "Nobody will notice your costume. You know Mother would have made you a whole sheep suit if she had time. Be a good sport. Please."

Ramona shook her head and blinked to keep tears from falling. "I told Daddy I wouldn't be in the program, and I won't."

"Well, OK, if that's the way you feel," said Beezus, forgetting to act like Mary. She left her little sister to her misery.

Ramona sniffed and wiped her eyes on her

hoof. Why didn't some grown-up come along and *make* her join the other sheep? No grown-up came. No one seemed to remember there were supposed to be three sheep, not even Howie, who played with her almost every day.

Ramona's eye caught the reflection of her face distorted in a green Christmas ornament. She was shocked to see her nose look huge, her mouth and red-rimmed eyes tiny. I can't really look like that, thought Ramona in despair. I'm really a nice person. It's just that nobody understands.

Ramona mopped her eyes on her hoof again, and as she did she noticed three big girls, so tall they were probably in the eighth grade, putting on robes made from better bedspreads than the shepherd's robes. That's funny, she thought. Nothing she had learned in Sunday school told her anything about girls in long robes in the Nativity scene. Could they be Jesus's aunts?

One of the girls began to dab tan cream from a little jar on her face and to smear it around while another girl held up a pocket mirror. The third girl, holding her own mirror, used an eyebrow pencil to give herself heavy brows.

Makeup, thought Ramona with interest, wishing she could wear it. The girls took turns darkening their faces and brows. They looked like different people. Ramona got to her knees and peered over the lower branches of the Christmas tree for a better view.

One of the girls noticed her. "Hi, there," she said. "Why are you hiding back there?"

"Because," was Ramona's all-purpose answer. "Are you Jesus's aunts?" she asked.

The girls found the question funny. "No," answered one. "We're the Three Wise Persons."

Ramona was puzzled. "I thought they were supposed to be wise *men*," she said.

"The boys backed out at the last minute," explained the girl with the blackest eyebrows. "Mrs. Russo said women can be wise too, so tonight we are the Three Wise Persons."

This idea seemed like a good one to Ramona, who wished she were big enough to be a wise person hiding behind makeup so nobody would know who she was.

"Are you supposed to be in the program?" asked one of the girls.

"I was supposed to be a sheep, but I changed my mind," said Ramona, changing it back again. She pulled out her sheep headdress and put it on.

"Isn't she adorable?" said one of the wise persons.

Ramona was surprised. She had never been called adorable before. Bright, lively, yes; adorable, no. She smiled and felt more lovable. Maybe pink-lined ears helped.

"Why don't you want to be a sheep?" asked a wise person.

Ramona had an inspiration. "Because I don't have any makeup."

"Makeup on a *sheep!*" exclaimed a wise person and giggled.

Ramona persisted. "Sheep have black noses," she hinted. "Maybe I could have a black nose."

The girls looked at one another. "Don't tell my mother," said one, "but I have some mascara. We could make her nose black."

"Please!" begged Ramona, getting to her

feet and coming out from behind the Christmas tree.

The owner of the mascara fumbled in her shoulder bag, which was hanging on a chair, and brought out a tiny box. "Let's go in the kitchen where there's a sink," she said, and when Ramona followed her, she moistened an elf-sized brush, which she rubbed on the mascara in the box. Then she began to brush it onto Ramona's nose. It tickled, but Ramona held still. "It feels like brushing my teeth only on my nose," she remarked. The wise person stood back to look at her work and then applied another coat of mascara to Ramona's nose. "There," she said at last. "Now you look like a real sheep."

Ramona felt like a real sheep. "Ba-a-a," she bleated, a sheep's way of saying thank you. Ramona felt so much better, she could almost

pretend she was woolly. She peeled off her coat and found that the faded pink rabbits really didn't show much in the dim light. She pranced off among the angels, who had been handed little flashlights, which they were supposed to hold like candles. Instead they were shining them into their mouths to show one another how weird they looked with light showing through their cheeks. The other two sheep stopped jumping when they saw her.

"You don't look like Ramona," said Howie.

"B-a-a. I'm not Ramona. I'm a sheep." The boys did not say one word about Ramona's pajamas. They wanted black noses too, and when Ramona told them where she got hers, they ran off to find the wise persons. When they returned, they no longer looked like Howie and Davy in sheep suits. They looked like strangers in sheep suits. So I must really look like somebody else, thought Ramona with increasing happiness. Now she could be in the program, and her parents wouldn't know because they wouldn't recognize her.

"B-a-a!" bleated three prancing, black-nosed sheep. "B-a-a, b-a-a."

Mrs. Russo clapped her hands. "Quiet, everybody!" she ordered. "All right, Mary and Joseph, up by the front stairs. Shepherds and sheep next and then wise persons. Angels line up by the back stairs."

The three sheep pranced over to the shepherds, one of whom said, "Look what we get to herd," and nudged Ramona with his crook.

"You cut that out," said Ramona.

"Quietly, everyone," said Mrs. Russo.

Ramona's heart began to pound as if something exciting were about to happen. Up the stairs she tiptoed and through the arched door. The only light came from candelabra on either side of the chancel and from a street-light shining through a stained-glass window. Ramona had never seen the church look so beautiful or so mysterious.

Beezus sat down on a low stool in the center of the chancel and arranged the baby's blanket around the flashlight. Henry stood behind her. The sheep got down on their hands and knees in front of the shepherds, and the Three Wise Persons stood off to one side, holding bath-salts jars that looked as if they really could hold frankincense and myrrh. An electric star suspended above the organ began to shine. Beezus turned on the big flashlight inside the baby's blanket and light shone up on her face, making her look like a picture of Mary on a Christmas card. From the rear door a wobbly procession of kindergarten angels, holding their small flashlights like candles, led the way, glimmering, two by two. "Ah . . ." breathed the congregation.

"Hark, the herald angels sing," the advancing angels caroled. They looked nothing like the jumping, flapping mob with flashlights shining through their cheeks that Ramona had watched downstairs. They looked good and serious and . . . holy.

A shivery feeling ran down Ramona's backbone, as if magic were taking place. She looked up at Beezus, smiling tenderly down at the flashlight, and it seemed as if Baby Jesus really could be inside the blanket. Why, thought Ramona with a feeling of shock, Beezus looks nice. Kind and—sort of pretty. Ramona had never thought of her sister as anything but—well, a plain old big sister, who got to do everything first. Ramona was sud-

184

denly proud of Beezus. Maybe they did fight a lot when Beezus wasn't going around acting like Mary, but Beezus was never really mean.

As the carolers bore more light into the church, Ramona found her parents in the second row. They were smiling gently, proud of Beezus, too. This gave Ramona an aching feeling inside. They would not know her in her makeup. Maybe they would think she was some other sheep, and she didn't want to be some other sheep. She wanted to be their sheep. She wanted them to be proud of her, too.

Ramona saw her father look away from Beezus and look directly at her. Did he recognize her? Yes, he did. Mr. Quimby winked. Ramona was shocked. Winking in church! How could her father do such a thing? He winked again and this time held up his thumb and forefinger in a circle. Ramona understood. Her father was telling her he was proud of her, too.

"Joy to the newborn King!" sang the angels, as they mounted the steps on either side of the chancel.

Ramona was filled with joy. Christmas was the most beautiful, magic time of the whole year. Her parents loved her, and she loved them, and Beezus, too. At home there was a Christmas tree and under it, presents, fewer than at past Christmases, but presents all the same. Ramona could not contain her feelings. "B-a-a," she bleated joyfully.

She felt the nudge of a shepherd's crook on the seat of her pajamas and heard her shepherd whisper through clenched teeth, "You be quiet!" Ramona did not bleat again. She wiggled her seat to make her tail wag.